The Rainy Day Puddle

By Ei Nakabayashi

It's raining!

Random House 🏠 New York

Translation copyright ©1989 by Random House, Inc. Illustrations copyright ©1984 by Ei Nakabayashi. All rights reserved under International and Pan-American Copyright Conventions. Published in the United States by Random House, Inc., New York, and simultaneously in Canada by Random House of Canada Limited, Toronto. Originally published as *Pichan, Bashan, Zabūn* by Fukuinkan Shoten Publishers, Inc., Tokyo. Copyright ©1984 by Ei Nakabayashi.

Library of Congress Cataloging-in-Publication Data:
Nakabayashi, Ei. The rainy day puddle. (Just right book) Translation of: Pichan bashan zabūn. SUMMARY: Little Frog's puddle grows bigger on a rainy day but becomes much more crowded as other animals come to join him. [1. Frogs—Fiction. 2. Rain and rainfall—Fiction] I. Title. II. Series: Just right book (New York, N.Y.) PZ7.N1398Rai 1989 [E] 88-19099 ISBN: 0-394-82095-9

Manufactured in Singapore 1 2 3 4 5 6 7 8 9 0

JUST RIGHT BOOKS is a trademark of Random House, Inc.

"Yippee! A puddle! And it's just the right size for me."

"Hi," says Tortoise. "Nice puddle."
"Sure is," says Little Frog.

It keeps on raining, and the puddle gets bigger.
"Howdy!" cries Crocodile. He jumps in too.

"Great day for a swim!" says Hippo. He joins the others with a giant SPLASH!

It's a good thing the rain has made the puddle so big.
Because here comes Elephant!

HOORAY FOR RAINY DAY PUDDLES!

"Uh-oh," says Elephant. "The rain's stopped."

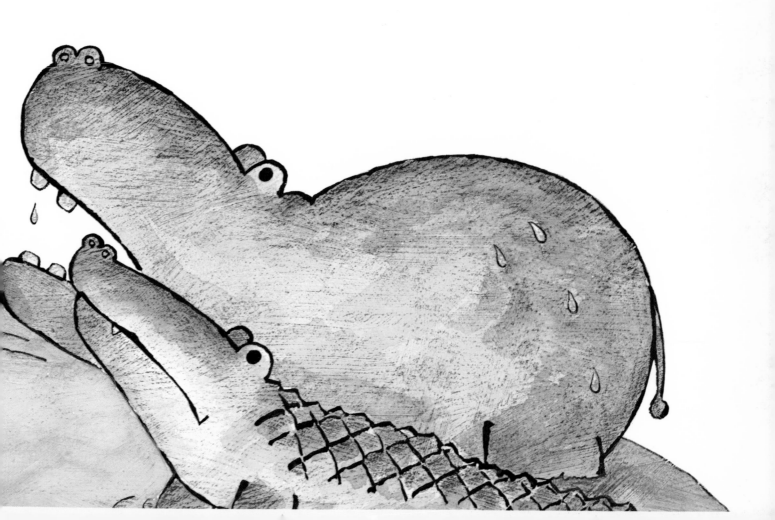

The sun starts to shrink the puddle,
so Elephant leaves.

When the sun makes the puddle even smaller,
Hippo goes too.

Then it's Crocodile's turn. "So long," he says,
a little sadly.

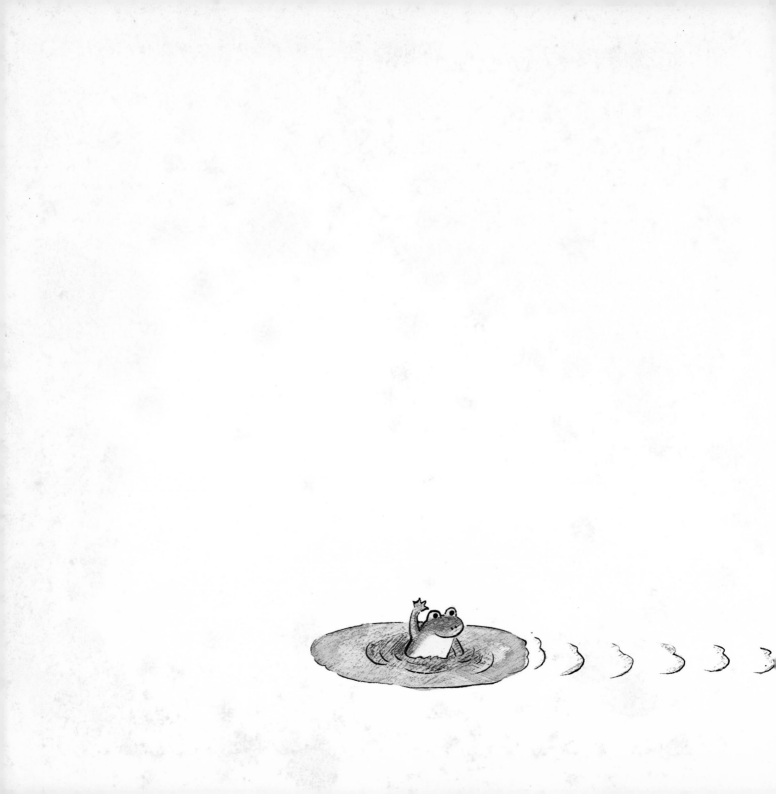